THE MEASLY VIRUS

Dedicated to Riley Hughes, a bright young life cut tragically short by a vaccine-preventable disease.

Part-proceeds from book sales will be donated in Riley's memory to the Princess Margaret Hospital Foundation to support Pertussis research and vaccination initiatives.

Published in 2015 by Watters Publishing
Suite 140, 315 Chiswick High Road, London, W4 4HH
www.watterspublishing.com

ISBN: 978-0-9933362-0-1

A CIP catalogue record for this book is available from the British Library.

THE MEASLY VIRUS

Written by Emma Vincent
Illustrated by Laura Watson

~ A Watters Publishing Children's Book ~

He's a menace that hides in plain sight...
I can't see him but I know that he's there,
he's evil and cunning and tiny,
and can fly on the dust in the air!

He enjoys hitching rides on buses
or travelling by train, plane, or car,
he's not fussy about how
he gets around but he likes
to roam wide and far...

And he's forever trying to catch me
because he's crafty and feels secure,
that he can invade my body
and make me feel sick
without any fear of a cure.

His plan is surprisingly simple...
to make my glands swollen and lumpy,
then give me a headache and temperature,
and make my skin itchy and bumpy.

So that while I lay sick and tired in my bed,
poorly and weak as a mouse,
this micro-monster is free to move on
and infect everyone in my house!

But if he catches my baby sister
or my Grandma who's frail and weak,
he could hurt them very badly
and make their futures' turn bleak.

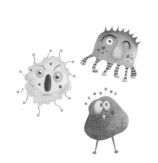

So I have a secret I'll share with you,
a plot to counter-attack!
And instead of becoming his victim
I've found a great way to fight back...

With a medicine called a vaccine
(which was given to me by a nurse),
that has strengthened my insides with
armour to defend me against his curse.

Now the mini-beast can't hurt me
because I have special protection,
for the vaccine has given me super powers
that fight his attempt at infection.

So no matter how hard he tries
to climb or clamber in,
he can't get inside my body –
he can't get under my skin.

I doubt he's feeling so smug now
his plans have all been wrecked,
and he can't survive long in the open
if he finds no-one else to infect.

So lets work together to beat him
and hand-in-hand we'll settle the score,
for if we're all vaccinated against him,
this monster can hurt us no more.

Riley's Story and the Importance of Herd Immunity

On March 17th 2015, a four-week-old baby named Riley Hughes lost his brief battle with Pertussis (Whooping Cough) and passed away in Perth, Western Australia. Riley, like other vulnerable new-born babies, was too young to be vaccinated against this disease and relied on herd immunity to protect him.

Herd immunity (or community immunity) is a concept that turns ordinary people into superheroes. Anyone can become a protector of society just by keeping up-to-date with their immunizations, and here's how…

Imagine that germs that cause vaccine-preventable diseases fall from the sky like rain, and when you get vaccinated, you get an umbrella. Now, while most umbrellas are strong and effective, there is the odd umbrella that has a hole and lets some of the germy rain through. Furthermore, for various medical reasons, there are some people for whom the umbrellas can't open at all, and there are also those who are too young and/or weak that simply can't hold an umbrella.

For all of these people - those with holes, those with closed umbrellas, and those too weak - it is the collective protection of the rest of the umbrellas (the community of umbrellas) that is protecting them from getting wet. Hence the more umbrellas there are, standing side-by-side together, the less likely everyone is of getting touched by the rain.

So, please be a superhero and keep up-to-date with your vaccinations. By being a society protector you can help to stop vaccine-preventable diseases from impacting not only the people you love and care about, but also those people (like Riley) who rely on community immunity.

Made in United States
Troutdale, OR
04/18/2024

19226492R00017